Duck Bills

Tracy Kompelien

Illustrated by Anne Haberstroh

Consulting Editor, Diane Craig, M.A./Reading Specialist

ABDO
Publishing Company

Published by ABDO Publishing Company, 4940 Viking Drive, Edina, Minnesota 55435.

Printed in the United States.

Credits
Edited by: Pam Price
Curriculum Coordinator: Nancy Tuminelly
Cover and Interior Design and Production: Mighty Media
Photo Credits: Digital Vision, Photodisc, ShutterStock, Stockbyte

Library of Congress Cataloging-in-Publication Data

Kompelien, Tracy, 1975-
    Duck bills / Tracy Kompelien ; illustrated by Anne Haberstroh.
       p. cm. -- (Fact & fiction. Animal tales)
    Summary: When the migration begins, Mally Mallard decides to travel by airplane instead of using her own wings to fly to her winter home. Contains facts about mallard ducks.
    ISBN 1-59679-933-1 (hardcover)
    ISBN 1-59679-934-X (paperback)
    [1. Ducks--Fiction.] I. Haberstroh, Anne, ill. II. Title. III. Series.
    PZ7.K83497Du 2006
    [E]--dc22
                                                                            2005024138

SandCastle Level: Fluent

SandCastle™ books are created by a professional team of educators, reading specialists, and content developers around five essential components—phonemic awareness, phonics, vocabulary, text comprehension, and fluency—to assist young readers as they develop reading skills and strategies and increase their general knowledge. All books are written, reviewed, and levels for guided reading, early reading intervention, and Accelerated Reader® programs for use in shared, guided, and independent reading and writing activities to support a balanced approach to literacy instruction. The SandCastle™ series has four levels that correspond to early literacy development. The levels help teachers and parents select appropriate books for young readers.

| Emerging Readers | Beginning Readers | Transitional Readers | Fluent Readers |
| (no flags) | (1 flag) | (2 flags) | (3 flags) |

These levels are meant only as a guide. All levels are subject to change.

FACT & FiCTioN

This series provides early fluent readers the opportunity to develop reading comprehension strategies and increase fluency. These books are appropriate for guided, shared, and independent reading.

FACT The left-hand pages incorporate realistic photographs to enhance readers' understanding of informational text.

FiCTioN The right-hand pages engage readers with an entertaining, narrative story that is supported by whimsical illustrations.

The Fact and Fiction pages can be read separately to improve comprehension through questioning, predicting, making inferences, and summarizing. They can also be read side-by-side, in spreads, which encourages students to explore and examine different writing styles.

FACT OR FiCTioN? This fun quiz helps reinforce students' understanding of what is real and not real.

SPEED READ The text-only version of each section includes word-count rulers for fluency practice and assessment.

GLOSSARY Higher-level vocabulary and concepts are defined in the glossary.

SandCastle™ would like to hear from you.

Tell us your stories about reading this book. What was your favorite page? Was there something hard that you needed help with? Share the ups and downs of learning to read. To get posted on the ABDO Publishing Company Web site, send us an e-mail at:

sandcastle@abdopublishing.com

Mallard ducklings are led to water by their mother as soon as their soft, downy feathers dry off after hatching.

4

Mally Mallard is swimming in the lake, minding her own business, when she notices a huge, gray object in the sky.

Young, down-covered ducklings cannot fly until they are about two months old and their feathers have grown in.

"Oh my, what is that?"
she cries.

"It's called an airplane. People ride in it
to go to faraway places," Daddy Drake
says. "Soon you will learn to fly just like
that airplane."

Ducks' bones are hollow, which makes their bodies lighter. That makes it easier to fly long distances.

Mally is amazed! She wants to start right away! Mally's dad shows her what to do. Then Mally practices until she is flying high.

In the fall, mallards build up a store of fat on their bodies. This provides them energy for the long flight south.

By the end of the day, Mally is very tired from all the flapping. She thinks that getting a ride on a plane sounds like a better idea than doing all this work!

Mallards eat wetland plants and grains such as wheat, barley, and oats. They also eat some insects and shellfish.

The next day, Mally goes to the airport and jumps on a plane. As Mally sits down in her seat, the flight attendant asks, "Would you like lasagna or steak for lunch today?" Mally orders both!

Mallards spend the spring and summer in the northern United States and Canada. They fly south for the winter.

After a few hours, the plane lands.
Mally is excited to get into the warm
Texas air. On the way off the plane,
the attendant hands Mally an envelope.
In the envelope is a bill for $200!

Ducks waddle when they walk. That's because their legs are short and far apart.

Mally uses all of her money to pay
the bill. She is very disappointed and
walks off the plane flat broke.

17

Mallards fly in flocks rather than alone. A group of birds is called a flock.

Mally's family arrives several days later, very tired from their long flight.

When Mally greets her family, she exclaims, "I will travel with you from now on!" Mally has learned her lesson after paying that huge bill!

19

FACT or FICTION?

Read each statement below. Then decide whether it's from the FACT section or the FICTION section!

  1. Ducks' bones are hollow.

  2. Mallards eat steak.

3. Mallards fly in flocks.

  4. A mallard's feathers grow in about two months after it is born.

ANSWERS
1. fact 2. fiction 3. fact 4. fact

Mallard ducklings are led to water by their mother as   10
soon as their soft, downy feathers dry off after hatching.   20

Young, down-covered ducklings cannot fly until   27
they are about two months old and their feathers have   37
grown in.   39

Ducks' bones are hollow, which makes their bodies   47
lighter. That makes it easier to fly long distances.   56

In the fall, mallards build up a store of fat on their   68
bodies. This provides them energy for the long flight   77
south.   78

Mallards eat wetland plants and grains such as wheat,   87
barley, and oats. They also eat some insects and shellfish.   97

Mallards spend the spring and summer in the   105
northern United States and Canada. They fly south for   114
the winter.   116

Ducks waddle when they walk. That's because their   124
legs are short and far apart.   130

Mallards fly in flocks rather than alone. A group of   140
birds is called a flock.   145

21

Mally Mallard is swimming in the lake,   7
minding her own business, when she notices a   15
huge, gray object in the sky.   21

"Oh my, what is that?" she cries.   28

"It's called an airplane. People ride in it to go   38
to faraway places," Daddy Drake says. "Soon   45
you will learn to fly just like that airplane."   54

Mally is amazed! She wants to start right   62
away! Mally's dad shows her what to do. Then   71
Mally practices until she is flying high.   78

By the end of the day, Mally is very tired from   89
all the flapping. She thinks that getting a ride on   99
a plane sounds like a better idea than doing all   109
this work!   111

The next day, Mally goes to the airport and   120
jumps on a plane. As Mally sits down in her seat,   131
the flight attendant asks, "Would you like lasagna   139
or steak for lunch today?" Mally orders both!   147

After a few hours, the plane lands. Mally is excited to get into the warm Texas air. On the way off the plane, the attendant hands Mally an envelope. In the envelope is a bill for $200!

Mally uses all of her money to pay the bill. She is very disappointed and walks off the plane flat broke.

Mally's family arrives several days later, very tired from their long flight. When Mally greets her family, she exclaims, "I will travel with you from now on!" Mally has learned her lesson after paying that huge bill!

GLOSSARY

bill. a list of costs or charges for items purchased

distance. the amount of space between two places

flat broke. completely without money

hollow. having an empty space inside

practice. to do over and over in order to learn a skill

store. a supply kept for future use

travel. to move from one place to another

wetland. a low, wet area of land such as a swamp or marsh

To see a complete list of SandCastle™ books and other nonfiction titles from ABDO Publishing Company, visit www.abdopublishing.com or contact us at: 4940 Viking Drive, Edina, Minnesota 55435 • 1-800-800-1312 • fax: 1-952-831-1632